Alley

by Claire Violet

illustrated by Susan Havice

An alley cat is a tough, little cat that lives outdoors in an alley,
the narrow lane between buildings.

Richard C. Owen Publishers, Inc.
Katonah, New York

Alley Cat chased a mouse.

Alley Cat chased a frog.

3

Alley Cat chased a bird.

Alley Cat chased me!

Then along came Zak.

He chased Alley Cat . . .

up a tree!